The Wheel Iz

Reid Pierpoint

Copyright © 2025

Artwork by Sarah Duke

This Book Is Gifted

To:

From:

_____

_____

_____

_____

_____

_____

_____

_____

_____

DEDICATION

This book is dedicated to the average young person.

I assure you, most of us are average in some way. We have our talents, advantages, and disadvantages, but the overwhelming majority of us humans fall into the extreme average. I say that not to discourage you, but to encourage you that you are not alone.

We live in extraordinary times. We have the most comfort of any point in human history, yet this only makes the harsh realities of life seem more unjust. If everything is better, why doesn't it feel that way? If we have everything we need, why do we still feel so discontent and like we need more?

Modern life has created an exciting, yet uneventful pace where the prescribed script seems to be simply to produce and consume. This leads us to deeper disconnections with ourselves, communities, and loved ones, and leaves us focusing mostly on our status and well-being. We chase entertainment and fear boredom. We seek to meet our own needs and fail to see the needs of others. It furthers us down the path of isolation and nihilism. It turns us into wounded critics and not the triumphant survivors we could be.

The cure we most often find is our work. It keeps us entertained, gives us constant feedback on the value we bring, provides us with resources, and allows us to compare ourselves to those around us.

May the best producers and consumers win. This striving to be successful in the eyes of our peers, or worse, the entire world, leads us to work harder for the signs of material wealth, accumulate debt, and put off long-term investing until we realize that we have wasted our lives focused on a false sense of meaning.

However, once we have had the chance to see this system for what it is, it is likely too late to fully recalibrate. We sustain losses to our finances, relationships, health, and our very potential for success and happiness. Resetting feels like moving backwards. It isn't, though. It is an important step forward. Surviving economically in the system that we call modern life is important, but it is playing life on easy mode. It is only one piece of a complete and meaningful life. Finding the balance between work, relationships, and personal growth is the only way to level up. It leads you to higher accomplishments than simply the material.

In the realm of personal and spiritual growth, never underestimate the power of ritual. Traditions and habits that become deeply ingrained in human behavior shape our future. Whether it is a moral framework, a societal expectation, a cultural norm, or just a daily rhythm, humans crave predictability. After all, that is the ultimate signal of security: the lack of surprises and knowing what is going to happen. Your habits will be indicators of your successes and failures, and your ability to integrate with others' proclivities will define your relationships.

Most importantly, in a world that is always changing, we should never place our entire worldview on one aspect of life. As we live and grow, we rarely find that things work out as we thought they would. We find that our core beliefs hold details that contrast with a straightforward definition of how things are. We cannot be broken by this, but must be strengthened. New and even conflicting information to our held knowledge is not a threat, but an opportunity. A chance to enhance our understanding and better apply it. True balance in our beliefs will be a defining characteristic of future morality. Too fluid, and we become indifferent to truth. Too rigid, and we are easily fractured.

I hope my words can help you see the threat in rigidity and the freedom in ritual. How a sense of duty is not imposed, but taken up willingly, and we are made better for it. How romance is not the purpose of love, and a lack of romance does not indicate a lack of love, support, or partnership. We all live in some kind of cage, but that does not mean we lack freedom. True freedom is realizing you have a choice, even if it has confines. The choice is to be grateful and contribute to the well-being of others or be resentful and work solely for our own ends. Your choice is not what cage you are in, or even who is in it with you, but how you coexist with them in an imperfect environment.

I hope I can inspire you to be courageous, because that is what the world needs. We need people who are courageous and steadfast to embrace their place in life and cooperate with others. We need those who are willing to work within the system with integrity to make it better, even when it doesn't feel like they are. We need those who are courageous enough not to change simply because it would be different, but because it creates a truly better model for the future, for everyone.

I am not suggesting that you be an obedient cog, but someone who understands the important role each of us plays in the machine that is our world. Cogs as we may be, we are driven by others' movements, and likewise, we drive others. Our effectiveness isn't based on our size, but on our efficiency and lack of unnecessary friction. The sharpness of our teeth and the number of other parts they touch. Most importantly, if one component stops, it can affect the entire machine until it is repaired or replaced. Broken systems halt all progress.

You are important and have important roles to play, but they require you to participate in whatever situation you find yourself in. You will have the opportunity to excuse yourself from life and retreat when things get hard. You can always go back to a life of simply producing and consuming, but value is found in how you face inevitable adversity, motonony, and your questions of meaning. Don't give up, press on, and grow. Realize you have immense value, and your greatest challenge will be to find where it fits in.

Thank you for reading

The Wheel Iz

CHAPTER 1

The light shifted from dim, yellow, evening tones to the bright, sterile white light that signified daytime in the shopping mall. The security guard's keys jingled as he made his morning rounds, unlocking the back doors as usual, prior to opening. The door slammed open and closed, echoing through the halls, almost rhythmically as the shopkeepers made their way into the mall to open their stores. Same as every day.

Nestled at the far end of the mall, near a large department store, was a small pet shop. The store was narrow, but went back some way to maximize the space. There was little use for a large storage area in the back. Most of the wares were displayed on racks up to the ceiling in two rows, extending all the way to the back of the store. The front of the store had a few cats with their tall scratching posts in cages. Lining one wall were three stories of curated terrariums with bright heat lamps, housing various species of reptiles. The other wall showcased even more aquariums filled with fish. Middle of the store, almost to the entrance, were two open-air bins. One for the two or three rabbits and guinea pigs, and the other housed a colony of mice. Undoubtedly, the rabbits near the entrance were strategically placed to capture the foot traffic of children wanting to pet the small, timid animals.

The mall was a busy place, with customers cycling through. It never failed that parents would leave their children unattended to watch the small creatures and attempt to touch or capture them for a closer look. No matter how busy, though, the schedule was all the same. The lights changed from dim to bright, the chain door rattled open, food was served, the animals dodged children, then the lights would dim again, the doors would lock, and things would begin to quiet down in the pet shop until morning.

The mouse colony was the life of the shop. It always seems to have more going on than any other section of the shop. This could have been due to their sheer numbers, since there were often two dozen or so living in the open enclosure. Even though the large area was divided into eight small cages by small plexiglass dividers, plenty of socializing was always happening. Most of the mouse families kept to themselves, though sometimes one would make it over the barrier and into another area, leading to romance or fighting. Regardless, it was a busy place.

One of the families was that of Gretchen. She was the mother of two girls and two boys, all about five weeks old and nearing maturity. The smallest and youngest boy was Izabel. Izabel was named, originally mistaken for being a girl on account of his smaller size, but his mother figured the name was still just fine. She wasn't the kind to fuss over things that worked as they were. She simply called him Izzy while his siblings called him Iz. Iz was timid, but curious. He played well with his sisters and was always excited to cuddle close with his mom and sisters as the lights dimmed for the evening. His size and demeanor kept him out of territorial squabbles that were common in the crowded spaces. By all accounts, he was very easily overlooked; no one saw him as a threat, and he liked it that way.

Every now and then, Iz and his sisters would start playing. It would be a game of tag or simple wrestling, but they would all run about and make such a ruckus, rustling through the cedar chips or slamming into the walls, that it would draw the

13

attention of customers coming into the store or even the shopkeeper. Their mother would quickly remind them to "calm down and be quiet so you don't end up like your father." The children never met their father. They knew of him only through the stories their mother would tell to instill in them fear and to keep them in line.

Just before they were born, Gretchen was in another cage with the children's father, Emil, and a few of their siblings. Emil loved attention from the humans when they would come in. While most of the other mice would run and hide, or even bite if touched, Emil would actively seek the attention of the humans. Originally, it was to draw attention and protect the others, but as he continued to have positive experiences with more gentle humans, he grew to like the attention. He also found that struggling led to much worse outcomes.

Emil's own brother had suffered a broken leg when he was picked up by a child. When trying to thrash free from the child's grasp, their grip around his little body became tighter. As he finally escaped the clenching hand, ready to make the jump back to the others, the child reached out and quickly grabbed, catching only his leg with a forceful grip around his tiny leg. The bone in his upper leg snapped, and he never walked again. After a day or so of limping and crawling about the cage, the shopkeeper gathered him up in a box. He was never seen again.

One day, a man came in, looked at the mice for only a minute, and shouted something to the shopkeeper, who quickly came and rounded up fourteen of the mice from various cages and slipped them into a box. Emil was one of them, but sensing something different, he was able to distract the shopkeeper enough to spare Gretchen, who was pregnant with their children. This man was different from the typical children or customers that the mice were accustomed to seeing. There was a smell about him that reeked of danger, as if he were accompanied by a predator. Then, as cold and quickly as he entered the shop, he was gone with the box full of mice. No food, no cage, just mice.

Gretchen speculated about what happens to all the mice who leave the colony. She tells her litter how small human children are prone to playing roughly and neglecting the mice they take as pets. If they wind up with a child too small, they will surely be stepped on or starved due to neglect. Worse, if they are picked up, they may be used in experiments or even as food. Where she collects such wretched stories always escapes her kids. When asked,

Gretchen simply attributes this knowledge to a group of mice brought in long before the kids were born. That group was conveniently gone and not able to confirm the tales. Regardless, Gretchen instilled a fear of being chosen by any human and encouraged all her children to keep their heads down and not go looking to be picked up by anyone.

Iz remained curious, though. He would scamper away and watch in awe from a distance as the giant humans came through and would choose mice from the cages at random. Sometimes one, sometimes two, but the amount of food and other items he saw leaving with them seemed to be more that of paradise than a death sentence. "Imagine having a whole cage to yourself," he would whisper to his sisters. "Imagine not having to fight for food or live in fear of being taken away to an unknown place. Wouldn't that be great?" he thought as a single mouse from another room was gathered up into a white box and whisked away.

CHAPTER 2

The lights cut to bright, and the slam of a door signaled the beginning of a new day. The siblings were cuddled together in the corner of their section of the bin. As they slowly began moving to greet the day, it came to Iz's attention that someone was missing. After looking around briefly, he noticed his brother Ivan was not in the cell. Acclimating to the day, he began to slowly look around as his vision cleared. He heard rustling in the section next to theirs. He heard giggles and what sounded like a typical bout of roughhousing. As he looked through the foggy plexiglass, trying to make out what was going on, he realized the source of the noise.

In the section on the other side of the divider was another group of mice: a mother and her three daughters. The two males who were in the section had been picked up a few days ago, and things had

19

been pretty quiet since. The daughters often played with Iz's sisters, Anna and Mary, with the barrier between them. They ran back and forth, trying to make out communications. The plexiglass divider made conversation difficult, but the motions by all the girls seemed to encourage jumping the barrier to meet. The barrier, however, was about eight inches tall, and when any of the girls tried to jump, they would only manage about two-thirds of the way before clumsily falling back into the wood shavings.

Every time the girls would play, Ivan would helplessly try to get the other girls' attention. He would run around the cage as fast as he could, bulk up to show his size, and even push over his sisters in a show of strength. Iz always found Ivan's behavior around the other girls to be ridiculous. Iz, for one, couldn't compete with Ivan when it came to size or physical ability. He had also never seen anyone clear the barrier, so what was the point? When all this was going on, he would simply take a nap or use this time for a good grooming.

Nonetheless, it seemed Ivan had done the impossible. Between pushing a pile of wood shavings together and what must have been the highest jump of his life, Ivan managed to make the leap and introduce himself to the sisters.

Iz got close to the glass, standing up to see a little more clearly through the foggy barrier. His brother approached the other side, jumped playfully, and taunted Iz with faces and lewd thrusting gestures. His taunting laughter was heard clearly over the barrier. "Come on, little brother! Too small to come where all the fun is?" Ivan jeered as the girls giggled. The three eventually tackled Ivan, and they ran off to the other side of the enclosure, obscured from Iz's view, where the rustling and giggling continued for hours.

"Well, I guess dreams can come true," Anna said rather snidely. "They can hump each other into oblivion," Mary added. Ivan was always driven by two things: food and the idea of humping any female he came across. Constantly, and often unintelligibly, he would make reference to all the pretty girls in the other cages. He would tout how the girls liked big, strong men, so he wanted all the food he could get to bulk up. He would always offer advice to Iz to "eat more so maybe you won't look so scrawny," "run and show the girls how fast you are," or "stop being so close to mom and the girls. It makes you look like a mama's boy." It really did seem like all that advice paid off for Ivan. He had made it to his own version of heaven.

"Could you even imagine some boy jumping into our home?" Mary pondered. "Someone coming in to steal all our food and expect us to just let them have their way with us. Disgusting. I am perfectly fine with Ivan and his pervy self trapped on the other side. I hope he stays stuck over there," she added. "I don't know," said Anna. "It may be nice to have a man around. No offense, Iz. They can't all be as annoying as Ivan." Iz wasn't particularly phased. He was used to knowing that he wasn't the model male and, in accepting that, he relinquished a lot of the desire to mate, especially at mass. He wanted connection, friendship. If anything, he wanted purpose. Even if the perfect girl was dropped into his cell, what is the point of pursuing those things when you are trapped in close quarters with your mom and sisters, he thought. Having all those women in one place. That is no way to live. More so, Ivan would probably just swoop in and bully Iz out of the situation, so it is best not to want those things. "Iz, I said no offense. Don't look so sad," Anna said as Iz slowly slunk off to his corner.

Iz imagined what it is like for those other mice that get taken away. If they are sent off in pairs, do they have deeper relationships? Do they get tired of each other? What if it turns out they hate each other?

I guess the only thing to do would be to endure it or fight to the death. "Maybe I *should* start eating more," he said out loud as he thought about the likelihood that most any average mouse, male or female, would likely best him in any fight. His sisters could, most definitely. Maybe being chosen as a single mouse is the best scenario for someone like him.

Maybe wanting more than a good place to sleep with plenty of food was foolish. A mouse's life shouldn't be that complicated, after all. All mice know where they sit on the food chain. That is why his mother is fearful, and Ivan is so reckless. Life was short, and their part in it was minimal. If he died alone in the wild or captivity, it wouldn't seem like it would make much of a difference. The impact he would have on the world would never be noticed. Still, he would prefer not to go out as a mere snack for some other creature. That seemed the most frivolous of all.

In all his thinking, he stood there, staring off far into the distance despite his small enclosure. His view wasn't so much with his eyes as his mind. His senses were dulled by his deep trance of pondering the questions of meaning and what his future held. Dulled so much that he didn't notice the shadow of a young human looming over his very section of the bin. Slowly, he noticed a large figure moving toward him. He snapped out of his trance, straight into a dazed disbelief of what was happening. The figure was a hand, just inches away from him, and moving closer. Iz had nowhere to go; he was frozen in his corner. The hand stopped moving and opened. Iz moved closer to smell it and get a sense for the god-like figure in front of him. He didn't smell predators; he didn't sense danger. He sensed calmness, even kindness. He got closer and found himself slowly stepping into the boy's hand. as he did, he was then lifted high above the enclosure. He heard his mother scream his name and saw her and his sisters below, panicking and running about in a frenzy. He saw his brother in the adjacent cell, popping up from a pile of wood shavings.

He felt the hand slowly tighten around his body, securely keeping it in place. With haste, he was quickly whisked away from the mouse bin and dropped gently into a little, white cardboard box. Snapping out of his disorientation and overcome with anxiety, Iz jumped from wall to wall, hoping to get the height or grip to scale the edge and blindly fall back into the soft embrace of a pile of wood shavings. It was no use; he was not big enough or strong enough. He stared up into the fluorescent ceiling lights one last time as the box top folded shut, leaving him alone in darkness, trying his best not to be thrown about as the container moved.

While he could not see, he could sense himself leaving the pet store. All the sounds he was used to hearing from a distance were now closer, louder. All the smells, crisper or entirely new. Slowly, everything was new and unfamiliar. He was now nowhere near the shop. With a slam of a car door, he soon found himself being lulled to sleep by the rhythmic sound of the engine, the constant vibration, kept awake only by a rush of light and the glimpse of the boy's eye peering into the box occasionally.

Chapter 3

The car came to a stop. Almost immediately, Iz was thrown to the side of the box as it was picked up and whisked out of the car. He braced himself as he was continuously jostled about whilst the boy raced up the stairs of their apartment building. The room was on the third floor, but may as well have been Mount Everest for a small mouse in a cardboard box, just trying to stay upright. Iz heard keys jingling, a door slamming, and fast footsteps before hearing another door shut and then feeling his box placed on a hard, stable surface. There were a few minutes of loud rustling and metal clanging as the boy assembled a small, budget cage that was soon to be Iz's new home, complete with a food bowl and an affixed water bottle. The cage had two doors, one at the top and a larger one in the front to make cleaning easier.

The top of the box opened slowly, and light

poured in. The boy picked up the box and proceeded to tilt it over the large front opening to the cage. Iz scraped his paws frantically, trying to gain some sort of grip to keep from falling out. He didn't know how far down it could be or where it would leave him. The cardboard box, all of a sudden, didn't seem so bad, and he was fine to stay there. The efforts were in vain. With a slight shake of the box, Iz lost what little grip he had and slid out. The fall was short; he landed on his feet, and beneath them, he felt the familiarity of wood shavings. He looked around and was amazed at the place he arrived in.

He could see all around him. It was a small room with a bed and a desk next to the bookshelf where his cage sat. What fascinated him the most, however, was the window next to him, in front of the desk. The light poured in. It was warm. Iz had never seen sunlight, growing up in the mall pet shop. He only knew the harsh fluorescent lights above the mouse bin. This was different, natural, and amazing. He stood for a second in awe of it before scanning the immediate surroundings in his cage.

There was a small plastic wall before the bars of the cage began. The wall was tall enough to obstruct the view of the base of the window that let the sun in, but still short enough that Iz could stand

and see over it. There was a food bowl, filled with more food than Iz could eat in a day. With no one to fight for food around, any primal concerns of starving quickly left him. The wood shavings were laid in a thicker layer than the bin ever was, leaving him feeling as if he was walking on clouds everywhere he went. He thought to himself, "This is paradise. I have everything I'll ever need. I wish my mom and sisters could see this, then they would really be jealous."

Iz spent the rest of the day in a state of awe. He ate more that day than he ever had in his life. He napped in the comfort of the sunlight in the plushest corner of the enclosure. He stared out the side of the cage and watched birds flying past the window against the bluest sky. He watched the boy, who tidied his room and sat down at the desk with books and pencils. The boy focused intently on his work at the desk in front of the window, getting up every now and again to pace about, talk to himself, and maybe get distracted by a toy or other item in the room.

As the day progressed, Iz noticed something peculiar. The light from the window began to dim and change colors. The once bright blue sky had now turned orange and pink. The warmth of the rays were no longer pouring in. The light was leaving. As the light left, the room grew darker until, abruptly, a light came from a single dim bulb on the ceiling. The dim light almost reminded Iz of the evening lighting when the mall closed, signalling a sleepiness in him, though he didn't feel the hour warranted a night's rest. Nonetheless, it lured him to a corner of his cage. It made him think of his family and how he wouldn't have anyone to cozy up next to tonight. Almost instinctively, he cleared away some of the plush wood shavings and made himself a slightly harder, more uncomfortable, but more familiar place to sleep. He lay down, not sleeping, but lethargic from homesickness. Just then, a voice called from the other room. The boy promptly stood up and left the room. Iz was left alone in the most quiet and still place he had ever experienced.

The light in the window continued to dim. The boy came in and rustled about, changing into pajamas. This snapped Iz out of his lethargic state, stricken with curiosity around the novelty of the boy changing clothes and thus his entire appearance for a distance. How amazing to an animal that will remain with the same color coat for its entire life. Mice aren't exactly concerned with originality, after all. After the boy changed, he turned off the light and went to his bed to sleep.

Darkness instantly engulfed the room. A

darkness that Iz had never experienced. Aside from some shadows from the moonlight, he couldn't see. Was he blind all of a sudden? "What is going on?" he thought. He froze in panic. He stumbled about awkwardly in the darkness briefly, but after bumping against the wall, he decided to stop and reorient himself. Taking a breath and acclimating to the reality of the darkness, he noticed something in the stillness. He could hear much more than he had noticed before. Car sounds outside, people talking in rooms or even streets away. He noticed that his whiskers felt all his surroundings with a heightened level of detail. He moved his face back and forth to feel the walls, the floor, and unusually thick patches of wood shavings. He started walking, feeling his surroundings, and was amazed at how fast moving through the darkness became easy, instinctual. He moved around, faster and faster for what seemed like ages, until he finally found his thick pile of wood shavings and fell into it. No longer fearing the dark and feeling quite accomplished for it, he fell off to sleep.

Life continued like this for days, then weeks. More food than he could eat, comfortable naps, observing the window and the boy, and then sensory seeking play at night. It became routine and unexciting quickly. Iz found myself wondering many times a day what the point of it all was. He wondered where the boy went each day after waking up and what he was doing with the books and pencils day after day. He wondered if the boy felt the same level of boredom as he did, doing the same thing every day. Perhaps what the boy was doing was wildly important; surely it had to be for someone of his size with the freedom to come and go as he pleased to be doing it so routinely. Iz knew the importance of the boy to him. Without him, no one would provide him food, which alone filled Iz with a high level of admiration for the boy's benevolence. Yet, each day was the same. The boy would come and go, then work until the light would begin to fade, then leave the room until he came back for bed.

Iz found himself becoming sluggish. He noticed that he was putting on quite a bit of weight. He noticed that his stints of running were starting to be shorter and that he was becoming slower, less agile. "I wish I had my sisters here to help me eat all this food. Even if there was less of it for me, at least I would have someone to play with after, and then maybe I would stay in shape," he said to himself. He had been talking to himself quite a bit recently. He tried to channel his thoughts into something like a conversation. Sometimes he would argue with himself over silly things or scold himself as his mother might. Even talking to himself started to lose its appeal after a while. "What's the point of talking or even thinking at all if there is no one around," he thought.

He wondered if he had his family back with him, if they would have anything left in common. They are probably all still playing games, cuddling at night, and continuing with life as usual. They probably didn't miss him anymore if they ever did at all.

Iz started to eat less. Partly a conscious notion to not eat himself sick and become so fat he could no longer stand on his hind legs to watch the window and the boy, but partly because he lost the desire to. He was caught between wanting to live better and wondering if he wanted to live at all. The days continued on still. More of the same, to where even keeping the routine was an arduously dull task. No reason to keep doing it, but no reason to stop.

CHAPTER 4

The days started to get shorter. It seemed like night came sooner every day. As the days grew shorter, the boy's time in the room grew shorter as well. Despite the shorter days, the boy still left his books as the sun went down and often didn't return until it was almost time for bed. The boy rarely left the light on, so no one noticed the reduction in daylight hours more than Iz.

One morning, the boy woke up, dressed, and left in the morning as he always did. Iz didn't particularly feel the need to watch. After all, he would come by to drop some food in the bowl soon anyway. Same as always. Lying around for a little while longer wouldn't hurt. However, the boy rushed out the door, not feeding Iz at all. This jolted Iz awake in panic. His bowl was nearly empty; surely he could survive the day, but there was a new question to answer: "How long will it be before the boy returns, and will he feed me then? What if it's days? I could starve!"

As the day progressed, the thought of food consumed Iz as he stared at the last few small pieces of the pellet food in his dish. He never felt so hungry as he did at that moment. Even though the food was right in front of him, he dared not touch it for fear that it would be his last serving ever. He finally succumbed, taking a single piece, eating it as slowly as he possibly could to savor it.

As he nibbled slowly at his food, he couldn't help but think, "Maybe the boy didn't feed me on purpose. I have become a little fat as of late, and I am not as active as I used to be. I have been pretty ungrateful. Maybe I don't deserve food. Maybe this is his way of getting rid of me." This wasn't how Iz normally thought, but the reasoning seemed sound in the moment. The boy used to watch Iz move about the cage, would occasionally hold him, and talk to him. With Iz grappling with his loneliness and questions of meaning, he hadn't been as entertaining. Maybe that was his purpose, and his failings are being punished. He could do better, he knew he could. If the boy would just come back and feed him, he would show him.

After pondering this in humble angst for what seemed like forever, but was most likely an hour, Iz heard the familiar sound of footsteps approaching the room. The boy came in holding a large plastic bag. He set it on the desk and quickly pulled out a container of food as well as another box. Iz was overcome with excitement to see the boy and began running back and forth, breaking to prop up on the side of the cage to see what the boy was doing. The boy opened the container of food and refilled Iz's bowl. Iz went straight for the food, starving since he spent the morning avoiding eating breakfast. As he was eating, he occasionally ran to the edge of the cage to see what the boy was doing since he was making quite a commotion with the box that he pulled from the bag he came in with.

The boy pulled a contraption from the box and began to work with the pieces. When all the pieces were out, he set the box next to Iz's cage. The box had an image on it that Iz couldn't help but be drawn to. The box was midnight blue, and on it, a picture of a mouse that looked much like Iz, running inside a wheel. There was an animated decal of a bright yellow lightning bolt that didn't seem like it belonged in the scene, but the background was a bright cityscape at night with hundreds of tiny lights shining in every window of the large buildings. On the box, a slogan read "Power your world!" Iz couldn't read, but he understood. He was inspired by the sight of another mouse, one with a job, with purpose, with ambition, with the power to make something happen.

The boy lowered a giant wheel into Iz's cage. One that looked identical to the one on the box. The center of the wheel had a black block from which a wire extended. The boy threaded the wire through the bars on the side of the cage and connected it to the wheel. Iz watched with much curiosity. The boy then placed a desk lamp on his table and ran the cord to the contraption, ultimately connecting the lamp to the wheel. The boy then flipped a switch on the block and reached into the cage. He spun the wheel a few times around, and the lamp on his desk slowly faded on. When the boy stopped, the light stayed on for a second and then slowly faded off.

Iz sat and stared in amazement, not fully recognizing the correlation. The boy then picked up Iz and put him in the wheel. Iz sniffed at it, investigating what this contraption could be. He moved a little, and the wheel turned, throwing off Iz's balance, so he quickly jumped out. The boy again picked up Iz and placed him in the wheel. This time, he slowly turned the wheel, forcing Iz to take a few steps. Iz kept taking steps, and the wheel kept spinning. The small steps quickly turned into a sprint, and then a full run. Iz noticed ahead that the light came on. He saw the picture of the mouse on the box. He realized that he was making things happen and continued on for a few minutes before hopping out of the wheel, feeling exhausted and accomplished. He rushed to the edge of the cage and, while panting, watched the light stay on another minute before fading out. The boy left the room as normal, and Iz was left to rest as the sun set.

The warmth of the sunlight and the softness of the pile of shavings felt more comfortable than just yesterday. His appetite was satiated despite only a small snack following his lack of breakfast. His body, while tired, felt revived. This feeling of contentment, happiness, was this purpose? Maybe this is what it felt like to be given meaning. Something to do that would benefit the boy, who has been so good to him, the one who provides him with food and a place to live. Perhaps this was the way to repay him. Iz's mind raced with pride and possibility until his tired body won out and he drifted off into an afternoon nap.

The boy arrived after a few hours, just as usual for the evening routine. However, this time, before sitting down with his books, he went to see Iz. He reached into the cage, picked up Iz and placed him on the wheel, and gave it a small turn to get it started. Iz ran happily. The light faded on as the boy sat down and opened his books, and took his pencil in hand. Iz ran for a few minutes, until he got tired. He slowed down, and as the light started to dim, he sped back up. He did everything he could to keep going as long as possible. When he finally couldn't go any longer, he jumped out of the wheel, exhausted and thirsty. He slowly made his way to the water bottle for a drink, and after a few laps of water, he propped against the edge of the cage, just in time to watch the boy scribble his last few notes before the light dimmed and went out.

As the light went out, the boy stood up, flipped the switch on the box off so that if Iz started running again, the light wouldn't come on. The boy then left the room without the normal call from the hallway. Iz again found his cozy corner and quickly fell asleep. He was so exhausted that he missed the normal nighttime routine and didn't wake up until the boy was asleep for the night. Iz ate a small amount, embraced some light evening activity, and went back to sleep, hoping this could be his new routine.

It quickly became a habit. His routine soon came to include keeping the light on for the boy as long as he could each day. When the light went out, the boy moved on, and Iz fell asleep, missing the boy's changing and going to sleep, but still getting some time in the dark and relaxation in the morning sun. It went on like this for weeks. Iz was getting stronger and was much happier with the newfound sense of purpose. He had never felt better. His loneliness and angst almost completely disappeared. This was his job, his new identity, and his reason to live. He talked to himself less, and when he did, it was positive. No longer did he feel the need to channel his mother's scolding. It was an occasional "what a beautiful day" or "today, we will go even longer than yesterday." He rarely thought of his family these days and never felt homesick. This was his home now. He had found his way and no longer needed support. He had the boy and the job he was given. He was needed and important. Iz was happy.

CHAPTER 5

Another new day had come. After weeks of his new routine, Iz was now able to keep the light going for more than an hour each night. A few times, the boy even got up before Iz was done, leaving Iz feeling very adequate and accomplished in his work on the wheel. His confidence and dedication had appeared to have reached their peak. He worked on his eating and sleeping habits to ensure he had the maximum amount of energy when the time came each evening to run. His body was now more broad and muscular. He was not the scrawny pup he was when he lived with his family in the bin, nor the overweight and slow version of himself before the wheel was added to his life.

As he woke and stretched, feeling his tightened muscles expanding, he said out loud, "Looking good. Those other mice back home wouldn't even recognize me now. Even Ivan would let me eat in peace if he were here." He decided to start the day with a few minutes on the wheel. The switch wasn't flipped, so the light wouldn't come on, but Iz would often go for a quick run in the morning, regardless. "Best to keep in shape," he would say to himself.

The boy approached the cage, opened the door, and dropped a handful of food in Iz's bowl. He watched Iz running on the wheel for a few seconds before chuckling and heading out of the room. Iz got down and stared out the window. Quite content with the life he had created. He felt more on equal terms with the boy now that he had something of value he could offer. The boy fed him and cared for him because Iz could keep the light on. The boy needed Iz to work; otherwise, he would have to do his work in the dark and wouldn't be able to see anything. It seemed like forever since Iz had seen the dingy light from the ceiling. Due to his new schedule, if the boy even turned it on, Iz was asleep and wouldn't wake up until late in the night, long after the boy had fallen asleep and the room was completely dark.

Iz was enjoying his midday routine of napping, eating, and daydreaming when he heard footsteps in the hall. Was the boy home already? That isn't usual. He wasn't due home for another few hours. Regardless, the boy came in holding a plastic bag and something else. He was also holding a familiar, small, white cardboard box. The boy set the bag down and carried the box over to Iz's cage. He opened the top door of the cage, then held the box over the front opening, tilted it, and gave it a few light shakes. Iz had flashbacks to his own experience, being lifted out of the bin, away from his family, the long, dark ride, trying to gain traction in the box to prevent himself from falling as the box shook, then falling into the cage he now called home. For a moment, he forgot about all the growing he had done and the confidence he had obtained. For that moment, he was still a tiny, scared mouse. He watched from the edge of the cage as a mouse fell from the box and landed in the middle of the cage. The new mouse stood stunned for a moment and then quickly panicked, running from side to side, trying to find somewhere to hide. They came face to face with Iz, shrieked, and ran to the adjacent corner and proceeded to bury themselves in a pile of wood shavings.

The boy watched for a minute to ensure that a fight wouldn't break out, but when he saw that Iz was stunned, but unoffended by the newcomer, and the new mouse was, clearly, not going to come out of hiding for a while, he decided to leave the room, but not before taking the cardboard box as well as the box from the wheel that still sat beside the cage with the image Iz fixated on during his runs.

Iz moved in closer to the pile of wood shavings, hiding the new mouse. "Hello," Iz said gently. "You can come out, I won't hurt you." As he moved in to assess the newcomer with a smell, he recognized the scent. It smelled a bit like the old pet shop bin. He wasn't positive, so he wouldn't immediately press that detail. The pile remained more or less motionless aside from the timid shaking of the scared little mouse. Iz continued, "You're new. I remember what that felt like. If you give it a chance, I think you'll find that things are pretty nice here. There is all the food you could ever want, the beds are so soft, and the view is amazing. I'd be happy to show you around." The mound remained still and silent. "Alright," said Iz, "I'll have to get to work soon. Help yourself to some food. The human is pretty good about refilling it for me since I help him out so much." With that, Iz went to his corner and lay down for a nap.

The boy came in a little later as Iz was waking up. The mound had moved some, but not enough to assume the new mouse had ventured out. The boy peered in for a second and then moved towards the desk, flipping the switch on the box. In an effort to be heard, Iz announced proudly, "Let's do this!" jumped onto the wheel, and started running. The lamp lit up, and the boy and Iz proceeded as if there was nothing new. A pair of eyes peered out of the mound of wood shavings, watching Iz run, focused and sure for what seemed to be an eternity. Finally, the boy got up, flipped the switch, and left the room. As Iz jumped down and headed straight to the water bottle, he commented out loud, "What a good night. We outlasted him again. That boy is slacking." After taking a sip of water and noticing the pair of eyes watching him, Iz called out. "Are you ready to come out yet? You can't stay in there forever." When no reply came back, Iz simply walked confidently back to his corner and plopped onto his pile of shavings. He closed his eyes and fell quickly asleep.

Iz awoke to rustling, but wasn't ready to open his eyes until he heard a thud and an exasperated grunt. He knew it was night and quickly assumed that the new mouse wasn't acclimated to the dark. "You have to use your whiskers," he said confidently, but sleepily. "What?" the voice called back. "So you *can* talk," Iz replied. "You have to use your whiskers to feel around at night. It is impossible to see, so you have to use your other senses. It is really fun once you get the hang of it." "Well, it isn't very fun now," said the voice. I have never experienced being blind." This affirmed more of what Iz smelled earlier, at least enough to assume this mouse may be from a pet shop as well. "I hadn't either when I showed up. Where did you come from?" he asked. "My cozy home with my mom, sisters, and lights that stayed on so you could see." Iz got up and made his way over to the new mouse at a normal pace, used to the darkness. He smelled more of the familiar scents as he got closer. He got close enough to brush his whiskers against the other mouse. "There you are," he said. "Try to be quiet and relax. You will need to stop trying to use your eyes and your other senses," he said. "Move your head side to side and feel what is around you." As they did, Iz moved close enough to be felt. The new mouse flinched and took a quick hop into the wall of the cage. "You might want to move a little slower until you get used to it," Iz commented. "Where are you trying to go anyway? Exploring is better in the daytime." "I need water, is there any here, or does that go away with the light as well?" the voice answered, frustrated. "It's over here, I will lead you to it, just get close and walk slowly, newbie," Iz said, closing the gap between them.

"My name is Abigail," she answered, "but my family calls me Abby." "And I'm Iz," he answered. "That's a funny name, but I feel like I have heard it before. Do you have a brother?" she asked. "Yeah. His name was Ivan. I haven't seen them in a long time. How would you know that?" he asked. "I was in the section next to you in the shop. Ivan jumped the divider and lived with us. I used to play with the girls from your section. Ivan watched you get taken away and tried to jump back over the barrier to your mom, but couldn't. It was for the best; he got two of my sisters pregnant. Anyway, he mentioned you every now and then and how we probably never noticed you because you were so small and quiet. You don't seem so small or quiet anymore." Still trying to move, Abby went on about how his family was still there, how her section was becoming crowded with Ivan's pups, and how life in the bin was exactly how Iz remembered it. "Well, it seems like everyone is happy and Ivan got everything he ever wanted," Iz said dismissively. While he was happy that everyone was ok, he wasn't thrilled that things seemed to turn out so well for Ivan. "Well, Abby," he said, trying to move on. "I need to get some sleep. If you'll be alright, I will get back to bed. Good night." With that, he moved back to his corner. "Goodnight then. I will figure it out," Abby said as she stumbled about in the darkness, trying to find her way back to a place where she could get some sleep.

CHAPTER 6

As the sun rose the next day, filling the room with light, Iz moved about the cage as if Abby wasn't there. He stretched, ran, got his water, and peered over the side of the cage as the boy got dressed. Abby, however, did not move. A long and fearful night in a new place did not allow her to sleep. She was also still used to sleeping in the light of the pet shop, so the sun did not wake her up as easily as it did Iz. When the boy opened the front of the cage and dropped a handful of food in the dish, his hand lingered and drifted over to pet Abby. At his touch, she immediately woke up and dashed to the other side of the cage. His hand followed, attempting to grab her, and as it got close, she delivered a warning bite. While she did not bite hard enough to draw blood, it did cause the boy to jerk back, almost knocking the entire cage over. He quickly withdrew his hand and closed the door. The boy finished getting dressed and left for the day.

"You shouldn't bite him, you know. He won't hurt you," Iz told Abby. "I don't know that," she said. "Why should I trust the human?" "Because he feeds us, cleans our cage, and takes care of us," Iz replied. "The least we can do is be grateful and nice. Suppose he stopped doing that. We would be left to starve. I am in here too and would prefer not to starve, especially because *you* bit him. So please, try to be nice." Abby went off in a huff back to the corner of the cage she claimed as her own. Annoyed, Iz went straight to the wheel.

After a few minutes, Iz hopped down and propped up on the side of the cage to stare out the window. Abby slowly approached him and looked out the window, too. "I'm sorry," Abby led with. "I am not used to all this yet. I miss my family, and I am tired. I had never slept alone before, much less in the dark. It was always with my family. I miss them. Even Ivan, as annoying as he could be." "Ivan was the last thing I thought I would miss. I guess you liked him, too, huh? Along with your sisters. I'm sure you all fought over him." Abby responded, "I guess, but it was more like a competition. He was the only male around, but whenever my sisters got pregnant, I sort of felt like I lost and then realized I may have actually won. He was pretty obnoxious after all." "Yeah, he was," laughed Iz. "I get it, though. Humans can be scary, but this one has been good to me. I owe it to him to do what I can to ensure he continues to feed and care for me. For us. We are now a team after all."

"Is that why you run on that wheel?" asked Abby. "Part of it, yeah," said Iz. "It's more than that, though. It makes me feel good, helping. Like I am doing something worthwhile and not just here to eat and sleep. The boy opens his books every night, and while I don't know what he is doing or why, I have to imagine it is important. The least I can do is help him by keeping the light on. I can do that. In return, I have all the food I can eat, a nice bed, and a good view. I don't have anyone else, so I do what I can for him." "You have me now," Abby replied. "We are a team after all." Iz smiled.

They talked for most of the afternoon. They talked about their childhood, their families, how the transition to this life went for Iz, and all the great things about it. They chased each other around the cage. Abby went to hop on the wheel, and Iz immediately shifted his mood. "Whoa," he said. "That is my job. It isn't just for anyone. I can't have you messing that up, so please just stay off of it." "Come on," Abby replied. "How hard can it be? You just get on and run." "No," Iz said more firmly. "This is my wheel and my job. That is my only rule." Sensing the tension around the conversation, Abby decided to leave that alone and change the subject. "Fine, but all your running only tires you out so you can't catch me," she said, giving him a friendly shove as she darted off. Iz quickly pursued her around the cage until he was too tired to continue and insisted that he take his afternoon snack and nap to be ready for the evening.

Iz slept. Tired from rambling about the cage all afternoon, he slept longer than usual, longer than intended, but still not enough. He woke up to the sound of the boy entering the room. Iz quickly jumped into action as the boy walked over to peer into the cage and flip the switch. As he sat down in his chair, Iz hurried onto the wheel. He ran faster than normal. The light quickly faded on. Iz quickly grew tired, but pushed on. He ran for a while before he jumped off the wheel and headed to the water bottle, panting. As the light faded out, the boy stood up and moved to look in the cage. Iz was finishing up his drink of water and looked at the boy. The boy's face appeared concerned, but mildly disappointed. He said nothing, but left the room as usual. Iz slunk back. Towards his corner. "That was impressive," squeaked Abby. "No, that was horrible," Iz said lowly. "I wasn't focused, I didn't pace myself. Worst of all, I should have kept going. I let the human down. Did you see the look on his face? I disappointed him. Just yesterday, he couldn't sit at his desk as long as I could run. I was useful, and today, I stopped him short."

"I thought it was fine. I certainly couldn't do that," Abby reassured him. "I'm tired from just our afternoon," she added. "Our afternoon!" Iz recalled. "That's it! I wore myself out playing with you all afternoon." It felt good to shift the blame. Perhaps Iz wasn't losing his touch; he just got distracted, and Abby was the one who distracted him. "Abby, we can't do that anymore. My work is much too important not to have the energy to perform as well as I can. The boy depends on me; if I don't keep the light going, who will? You have to let me save my energy." "Ok," Abby said, feeling the weight of Iz's conviction while still not understanding the reasons. She hadn't had time to appreciate the excess food or the soft beds. She only saw the bars of the cage and the darkness at night. She was afraid of the human's touch. If she were honest, she would just assume the human not be there at all. She was still reeling from the separation from her family. Who was to blame for that? The human. All of it. The darkness, her fear, her loneliness. Still, he placed her with Iz, surely, there was some reasoning for that. Surely fate had a hand in all this. As she stood, taken aback by Iz's devastated mood, Iz turned, crept back to his corner, and went asleep.

As night settled in and the sun went down. When the boy turned out the dingy overhead light and the room was dark, Abby grew fearful in her corner. She was lonely, so she crept over to Iz and lay close to him, slowly scooting until their backs touched. Iz half woke up from the feeling of someone near, he realized it was Abby, and thought for a moment about getting up in protest to her role in his poor performance this evening, but he didn't. He stayed. In fact, he stayed the entire night, skipping his late-night activity to ensure Abby's comfort. He found it nice to be cuddled next to someone again and feel part of a family. He thought back to his old place in the bin, cuddled up with his mother and sisters. He thought about Ivan and how he taunted him and wished he could see him now, bigger and stronger than he ever dreamed. He thought about Abby and how she still seems to have some fond feelings for Ivan. He also thought of how she must feel, new to the cage and missing her family. The least he could do is try to be kind; surely she will come around and enjoy it here as he does. Maybe one day, she too will come to appreciate the human. Just maybe they can live together happily.

CHAPTER 7

Abby started to acclimate to her new life. She fell into routine. Mainly, she based hers on Iz's, but it worked for her. She spent her days basking in the light of the window. She was less enamored with the boy and his comings and goings, leaving her to focus mainly on the world outside the window. She imagined what life would be like out there. She would close her eyes and just listen to the sounds and picture herself in the midst of the world and interacting with all manner of different creatures. Particularly interesting mice.

Abby and Iz spoke numerous times a day. Sometimes, about what they would see out the window and what they imagined was on the other side of the glass. Sometimes it would reminisce about their childhood, putting pieces together and cuing each other in on different perspectives of the same events. That made it feel like they had grown up together, though oppressively separated by the thick, foggy plexiglass barrier.

As these conversations went on, Iz had a tendency to land on how happy he had become here and how grateful he was for the boy and the comfort he provided. By this time, Abby would end the conversation in her mind and appear present to avoid a scolding from Iz. She still wasn't grateful for the human. After all, he took her away from her family and home and placed her here. Not that the abundance of food wasn't nice, but despite it being less at the pet shop, she always felt she had enough. Besides, in the bin, the shopkeeper never forgot to feed them, whereas the boy had skipped a few feedings recently. The comfort of the beds was nice, but she missed the warmth and connection of being close to those she loved.

That is what she missed the most: her family. The excitement that they brought kept her from being bored. If things got too quiet, one of her sisters would start a squabble, without fail. The three of them could never sit in peace and quiet for too long. It kept her occupied, and it kept her mind from wandering, which is all it seemed like her mind got to do these days. Strangely enough, she missed Ivan a bit as well. Not necessarily in a romantic way, but almost like a brother. Abby had spent the first few months of her life with her brother and her father in their section. They made her feel safe. In one of the adjacent sections, there were four males. One day, she heard a loud commotion. A fight had broken out between two of them, and one killed the other. She watched the fight through the foggy, distorted glass, so she couldn't make out the finer details of the fight, but she could make out the blood that resulted. She was mortified, but her father told her not to worry. While some males can be dangerous, he and her brother could protect her. He would joke that he was the biggest, scariest mouse in the whole building. She didn't see him that way, but believed him and felt safer for it.

After her Brother and father were taken, Abby's family feared and ran from any human interaction. Their section of the enclosure had a lip from the top of the bin that provided a strip of shade a little more than two inches from the wall, hidden from the view of most who would look in from above. If they sensed any humans, they ran into the shadows and burrowed as deep as they could to avoid being seen.

Then one day, early in the morning before anyone was awake, she heard a thud, and there was

Ivan. No warning, he was just there with a sly, but aloof look on his face as he confidently announced his presence with a "good morning, ladies." Her family cautiously huddled together, preparing for a fight over whatever it was he wanted, but he quickly disarmed with a stupid wink and said, "Don't worry, I'm a lover, not a fighter." They let their guard down, and in all the excitement, biology, more or less, took over. The sisters fought for Ivan's attention however they could, but knowing Ivan only wanted one thing, it wasn't a battle of wits. Eventually, Abby gave up. Her sisters were better built, and after a go or two, Ivan clearly preferred them over her. She wasn't overly disappointed, though. By the time the novelty wore off of having a male around wore off, he was pretty annoying. However, she could still talk to him like she did her brother, despite a never-ending string of innuendos, and she knew that if any of the more hostile males were to land in their area, Ivan would protect them, if nothing, out of blind chivalry.

Ivan had mentioned his brother, Iz, a few times. Normally picking on him for being sensitive or always thinking and trying to be smart, but it was only because he was too small to compete with Ivan. Abby found it curious how a bombastic male like Ivan could have a more thoughtful and sensitive brother. It kind of sounded nice and more like her father, but never seeing Iz close to the glass, his existence fell into obscurity, and then he was taken away.

Meeting Iz, she could see how that could have been true in his youth. She could still see the kind and sensitive nature of him. She could also see the spark of curiosity, but she was disappointed with his zealous tendencies towards the human and the wheel. It was as if all his curiosity was captured by fear and replaced with mindless devotion to a being that didn't necessarily care for them. Still, seeing that sensitivity and practicality were endearing and still in there. She never felt Iz was a threat, even in his lecturing and prophetic moods.

Abby was practical. She knew that she wanted a connection with someone else; she needed it. She also knew that this would likely be where she would spend the rest of her life, and he is the only other mouse she will ever be with. This gave her great incentive to try to bring the best out in Iz, not for him, but for her. She wasn't as sure that she wanted to spend her life competing with a human and wheel for attention, but didn't have a choice. The best option she had at this time was to keep the peace and support Iz, even if that meant going along with some mild insanity on occasion.

She was grateful on some level after all. She was grateful that she didn't end up here with a male that she felt would harm her, or worse, alone. She was grateful that she ended up with someone familiar. She was grateful that fate brought her to someone other than Ivan, whom she could have easily had to resort to starting a family with if she were left in the bin. She wasn't entirely ungrateful, no. She was also determined to make the most of her situation and find a way to be happy here.

CHAPTER 8

Iz had finished up his evening work on the wheel. The boy got up, flipped off the switch, and left the room. Iz was at the water bottle, rehydrating, when he turned to Abby and said, "That was a good night. I think the boy and I were in sync. We both held on a little longer than normal. Good work, indeed." Abby smiled and offered her encouragement, "You really are great at that. He is so lucky to have you." After the last week or two, Abby had started a habit of acknowledging Iz's work and contribution, and Iz saw that as accepting his role and importance here. It kept his mood good and minimized friction, allowing him to speak more freely and openly with her, keeping her from being too lonely. They both knew some of how the other felt and found this a fine compromise to living together happily. They were living together and coexisting as happy cellmates, making the most of this life.

As Iz finished his water, he said, "Well, I am off to my nap. Normal evening exercise?" "Of course," Abby said. "See you then." With that Iz went to his bed, plopped down, and with a satisfied sigh fell right to sleep. Abby watched the sun go down. She watched the boy come in and turn on the ceiling light, and get ready for bed. As he turned out the light and fell asleep, she quietly moved over to Iz's corner.

Abby nuzzled Iz, stirring him enough to move, but not wake up. She nuzzled his stomach, stirring him further. "Hi there," Iz said in a sleepy voice. "Time to get up already?" Abby nuzzled one more time and backed away. "Only if you want this," she added in a quiet, teasing voice. "Iz opened one eye to see Abby in the moonlight, provocatively positioning herself and clearly hoping to get Iz's full attention while eliminating any questions of what she meant." Iz stood up, led fully by his biological self at this stage. He moved over to Abby and slowly and carefully positioned himself. "Ok," he said quietly, yet excitedly, as he started.

This was an entirely new experience for Iz, one that he had given up on a long time ago, even to the point that while Abby had been with him in the cage for some time, the idea hadn't crossed his mind in much seriousness. It felt nice. He could see the appeal, and his body was on autopilot.

All of a sudden, Iz saw Ivan in front of him. He saw Ivan doing that stupid humping gesture that he was doing towards Iz the day he jumped over the wall. Iz imagined Ivan and Abby together. Immediately, Iz jumped back. "Something wrong?" asks Abby. "No, nothing. That was amazing," Iz said rather hurriedly. "You're done?" Abby continued. "Oh yeah. That felt so good," Iz said, falling back and facing the other way to avoid any inspection. Abby fell beside him. "I am really happy to be here with you, Iz," she said. "Really, of anyone else that I could have ended up with in this cage for the rest of my life, I am glad it is you. You are kind and intelligent, big and strong, pretty handsome, too. I am pretty lucky." Iz had never thought about it like that before. They were locked in a cage for the rest of their lives together, just them, forever. Forever with him being compared to Ivan.

Iz sat for a few minutes in silence, pondering all this. He tried to quickly reason his way out of these feelings. "Ivan is not here now. I am bigger, stronger, and smarter than Ivan ever was. This shouldn't matter," Iz thought. Iz thought of everything. Every possible and logical reason why he should set all those thoughts to the side and just be with Abby, but no matter what he tried, the taunting image of Ivan was there as if to block any potential view of the future. He thought of how he truly did like Abby, maybe even love her. He thought about what she said, how they would be locked in here together forever. He even thought of how miserable forever would be if he rejected her.

As these thoughts raced through his mind, Abby nuzzled close and said, "Your heart is still racing. What are you thinking about?" Iz gathered all his thoughts and feelings, quickly calculated everything he could say in this moment, closed his eyes, and with a deep breath said, "I love you." Abby raised her head, almost startled. She wasn't expecting that. The thought of love hadn't crossed her mind; more of a desire for closeness. She quickly weighed her responses and said, "Good... I love you, too." With that, they just lay there quietly for the rest of the night, each aware of the other's silence despite being awake.

Their thoughts moved from the event of the evening to the words they said. They searched themselves to see if they meant it or if moving into this territory was a good decision. They both agreed with themselves that it was. They did have a connection, there was a level of attraction, they liked each other's company, they were locked in here forever. It seemed only fitting to try experiencing love as opposed to any other feelings. It gave them a reason to be closer, it gave Abby a sense of connection and purpose she was looking for. It gave Iz a reason to focus on something other than the wheel, something deeper in his own life. This could be a great thing for them both.

From that night forward, they always slept together. They adopted calling each other "dear" or "honey." Their conversations hardly changed. The subjects remained the same. Their routines remained as well. For the most part, nothing in their lives changed at all, but that night it completely changed. They were happy, but accepted that they were trapped in a cage. They made the most out of their fate, but it was not freedom. They were held together by captivity and by making it work.

They were kind to each other, but distant. Friendly, but shut off. Neither had the heart nor the motivation to explore their lackluster romance. After all, this was life in captivity; creating too much of a fuss could be what made that reality unbearable. They owed it to themselves and to each other to keep things as cordial as possible, so they did.

CHAPTER 9

Days went by, and routine dominated the lives of Iz and Abby. Every day is like the one before. Pleasantries and food in the morning, afternoon nap, work in the evening, another rest, nighttime activity session, and then the same tomorrow. They were neither dissatisfied nor fully content. Their relationship had changed their routines to a strict regimen, and any deviation would send them into a disoriented frenzy of panic. One day it was raining, this meant that the day was dark and they both slept until the boy opened the cage to feed them, this led to a rushed breakfast. Abby commented on the dreary weather and lack of sunlight, leading Iz to accuse her of complaining too much. They spent the rest of the afternoon avoiding each other, sulking about the cage until Iz apologized. Abby reciprocated, then they simply went back to the normal activity.

That small argument was the most interesting thing that happened for the next two days.

Iz's daily run on the wheel was robotic, with no excitement to start or stop. He stopped keeping score of who lasted longer each session, him or the boy. Iz would no longer warm up or touch the wheel throughout the day; it was simply for the evening ritual.

Abby started napping during Iz's evening wheel time. He no longer ran with passion or excitement. One day, she simply dozed off to the sound of his droning footsteps and the rhythmic sound of the wheel and didn't wake up until nightfall. Once that happened another time or two, she realized that it just made sense, and she would be rested when Iz woke up at night.

Neither was passionate about much. They moved more slowly. Abby put on weight from not exercising. Iz talked less and less. The two had exhausted almost all conversation topics, and the most excited they could get about anything was a spat and an apology. They no longer spoke of dreams or what was beyond the glass, because there was no point. They no longer talked about the past because they had already shared every possible story multiple times. They just passed each other through the day with a smile and a light touch, then carried on in their own worlds.

One night, Abby had an idea. It was not a new one to her. She found herself thinking of it more often in her days of solitude with Iz. "Iz, why don't we have children? We could. I have always wanted a litter of my own, and it may bring us some excitement. Think of how much fun it would be to have pups running about with us." Iz was completely neutral to the idea of being a father. He never knew his father and wouldn't know where to start. What would that mean for his work? The children would certainly get in the way of that. Nonetheless, Iz agreed that life had become stagnant and that it would be a good way to liven things up. It certainly would make Abby happy. So he agreed calmly with a, "Sure, why not?"

They rarely embarked on intimacy. Iz, while he had mostly gotten over his issues with Abby's past, he had settled into sex not being a key part in their relationship. Any time they happened into an evening of sexual activity, it was at Abby's explicit request and quickly over. Trying to have a litter would require more effort.

They put in the effort, adding a few moments into the nightly routine to try. Still fast, but now lacking passion from both of them, it was clinical and repetitious. It was a job. They continued for days. Hoping the signs that Abby was pregnant would soon appear, but after a few weeks, they didn't, and that frustrated Abby immensely. Her mood seemed constantly tainted by disappointment. She was disappointed with Iz for not being more eager. She was disappointed in herself for not pushing for this earlier. Most of all, she was fearful that it might not happen.

This became a point of tension between them. Iz, in his clueless nature, would ask benignly, nearly every day, "Feel anything yet?" After a few days of this, Abby became so annoyed that her new response became, "No, do you?" Even the most clueless male could read that clue. Iz asked less frequently.

One night, as they lay down to sleep, Abby was crying quietly. Iz knew why. He, too, had started to feel a deep disappointment from trying and not seeing results. In an attempt to comfort her, he said, "It will happen, dear. Sometimes, I guess it just takes longer than others. If we need to pause trying, we can. This is hard on both of us." Abby said nothing. Just moved in closer and stopped crying.

After that, they stopped trying every night. They would occasionally, which made the pressure less intense. It also lowered each of their expectations. For the first time since they were together, they actually seemed to enjoy it. Iz stopped asking entirely, but noticed when Abby would be searching for a new feeling with mild enthusiasm, but quickly shift to a feeling of disappointment. Her head would hang low for a moment, and she would close her eyes, take a deep breath, and come up composed again. The cage was much too small for Iz not to notice.

At those times, he would move closer to her and offer an embrace. He didn't like seeing her feel that way. He felt more ongoing responsibility, wishing he could do more. In a way, this disappointment drew them closer. The heartbreak and inadequacy they were feeling required a level of support. In their situation, they each knew that the other was all they had. To leave someone alone with that pain was inhumane.

After a few more weeks, the pain dulled. Normalcy set in. The routine reset, and they went about it robotically. They cuddled more. They grew kinder to each other. They showed love and care for each other as they hadn't previously. They truly felt love.

Chapter 10

It was the most beautiful day. The sunlight came in through the window brighter than usual. The warmth of the rays was like a warm blanket. The kind of day that could lift the spirits of anyone. Abby woke up, stretched, and smiled. She got up and went straight to look out the window. A few minutes went by, and Iz was still fast asleep. "That isn't like him," Abby commented to herself. "It's a beautiful day, and he should see it." She went to wake him with a gentle nuzzle and shake. He stirred and slowly opened his eyes. Realizing it was well into the morning, he noted, "Wow, I must have really been out. Thanks, Abby. I was missing a beautiful morning." They spent the better part of the day staring out the window and watching the birds.

They went about their morning slowly. Despite the inspiration of the beautiful day, Iz was quiet. It seemed as if he was a million miles away. "Are you ok, dear?" Abby asked him. "You just seem off today. Iz shook out of his daze. "Oh yeah. I'm fine. Maybe I'm just a little tired. Who could be sour on a day like today?" It seemed as fair a response as any, and she didn't think much more of it.

They continued through their morning, and Iz went to lie down for his afternoon nap, but it was a little earlier than usual. He walked slowly towards his bed, not saying anything, lay down rather slowly, and with a deep exhale, he appeared to fall asleep immediately. He slept the remainder of the afternoon.

As evening approached, Iz was moving about, getting ready for his evening on the wheel. He stretched as the sun went down. He heard the boy's familiar footsteps in the hall, and Iz moved next to the wheel, at the ready. The boy entered the room, went straight to the switch, and sat down. Iz hopped in the wheel and started running. He ran for a minute and found it hard to catch his breath. A metallic taste filled his mouth. He slowed down. As he slowed down, the light began to dim. The boy looked at the light then turned and looked at the cage, making eye contact with Iz, who was now pushing forward to keep pace. The boy's face drifted back to the books.

Iz ran a little longer, conscious of his breath and the parchedness in his mouth. Then his vision seemed to go black for a moment, though it appeared he was still running. When he regained sight, he saw the light dimming. He lost balance and fell off the wheel. Abby was sleeping, but awoke to the sound of Iz falling to the ground. By the time her eyes found him, he was standing beside the wheel, panting. His eyes fixated on the boy, who was getting up from his chair. The boy passed slowly by the cage, inspecting Iz and the wheel, but without stopping, he passed by the cage and moved to the wall. Still facing the desk, the boy reached out his arm and flipped the switch on the wall. The ceiling light came on, and the boy sat back down and resumed his focus on the book.

Iz stared at the light. It had been so long since he had seen it on, he had forgotten about it. Iz's hind legs collapsed. His eyes were still staring at the hazy and dim light on the ceiling. His front legs quickly followed, and he fell to his side, still staring at the light. A tear rolled down his cheek as Abby rushed to his side. The world was blurry in the periphery of his fixated gaze. Abby's voice seemed muffled as she repeatedly called his name. He heard, but couldn't acknowledge her.

Finally, as things began to refocus, he simply muttered, "he never needed me at all." Abby paused. She had known this for some time. She knew the boy turned on that light every evening to get ready for bed, but Iz was always asleep, exhausted from his runs. His routine had insulated him from the truth that he used to know. She knew now was not the time to point this out, so she offered a comforting, "Of course he does, dear. He just saw how exhausted you are. That light is not nearly as bright as yours, but he knows that he simply needs to make due tonight while you rest. He is looking after you." Iz couldn't believe that. "No," he said, "I failed. He could have been using that the entire time. He never needed me. It was all for nothing." Abby's heart broke to hear him speak like this; the confidence and zeal had completely left his voice, as if his very spirit had been taken away with his strength. "I'm tired," he said. "Would you help me up so I can go lie down in my bed?" Abby helped him up and escorted him slowly to his bed of wood shavings. He laid down and, with a deep exhale, he closed his eyes and repeated, "it was all for nothing."

Abby watched him for a while. He twitched and whined in his sleep. He had never done that before. She wanted to be with him, but knew he needed space to process things, so she lay in her old corner, watching in disbelief at the broken Iz try to sleep. As he seemed to quiet down, she drifted off to sleep herself.

She woke a short time later to see Iz staring out the window into the night. She went to his side and asked quietly, "How are you feeling? That was quite the scare." "There are so many stars in the sky. It's amazing. Do you think anyone would notice if just one went out?" he asked. "I think each of them means something to someone," Abby answered. "Maybe everyone wouldn't notice, but someone would definitely miss even one star if it went out." "If most wouldn't know that it was gone, it probably wasn't that important," he said sadly and slunk back to his bed.

Iz slept through the morning the next day. Waking only when Abby nudged him, encouraging him to eat breakfast, Iz insisted he wasn't hungry and continued to lie there. Despite Abby's repeated attempts, this went on for two more days. Iz wouldn't talk, he wouldn't eat. Each evening, the boy flipped the switch and peered into the cage. He would reach in and gently pet Iz, but Iz remained still. Following a sigh, the boy flipped the switch off and instead turned on the ceiling light to work.

The next morning, Abby went to wake Iz up. "Good morning. I wish you would talk to me. I miss you," she said. "I should have been nicer to you," Iz said. "I let so many things get in the way of us. First, it was jealousy of Ivan. Then it was a fear of knowing that we would be in here forever, and then there was that stupid wheel. That wheel saved me one time, you know. It gave me purpose, a job when I was lost and feeling useless. I loved the boy and thought he loved me for what I could do for him, but it was never true. He only gave me a job to entertain me, not because I was useful. I gave up everything for him, my days, my energy, my love. All for nothing." "You are great to me, Iz," said Abby. "I am so glad that I ended up here with you. You are kind and strong. You love me, I know that. He stopped her. "But I could have been better. I should have been better. I'm sorry," he said. He closed his eyes and exhaled deeply again.

Abby wiped a tear from her eye and stood up, starting to move away. She hoped a perky tone and a task would get him moving. "Why don't we spend the morning together. Let's start with breakfast. What do you say, Iz?" No answer followed. No movement. "Iz, are you going to answer me? Let's get moving," she said, turning back. He just lay there. As she got closer, she realized he wasn't breathing. Her heart sank. She dropped her head. While she wasn't expecting him to just die, she couldn't help but feel unsurprised.

"How could you do this to me, Iz?" she said. "How could you leave me alone like this? We were supposed to be a team. We were supposed to have pups. Instead, you are leaving me alone. I've got no one now. Who will I talk to? Who will stay by me at night? You selfish fool and your stupid wheel. Your love for that stupid human. What about me? What am I supposed to do now?"

Chapter 11

Iz's lifeless body lay on his bed. For hours, Abby stared at him, contemplating what life would be like now. As the sun was just starting to go down, the boy came in. He peered in the cage as he passed. He paused, then came in for a closer look. He noticed Iz and sighed. Abby didn't move or acknowledge his presence; she remained in her corner, fixated on Iz's body. The boy opened the front cage door and reached in to pet Iz, but quickly realized the state of the little mouse. The boy slowly turned and left the room.

Abby wasn't paying much attention, but couldn't help but notice that she didn't hear the room door close. Wait, she didn't hear the cage door close either. She quickly stood up and looked to confirm what she thought. Sure enough, the front cage door was left wide open, and through it, she saw the door to the hallway open as well. Without any further thought, she leapt over the plastic sidewall of the cage and onto the bookshelf. It was a reasonably high series of jumps, but she spotted a clear path from the bookshelf to the table, to the chair, then to the floor leading out. Without hesitation, she ran and leaped, then again and again. Before she knew it, she was on the floor.

She headed straight for the door. She noticed a hole in the wall where a power outlet once was, just on the other side of the narrow hallway. She crossed the hall and leaped straight into it. She sat in the darkness, heart racing with a clear line of sight to the bookshelf where the cage sat. She heard the boy's footsteps coming back. As he entered the room, she noticed a small, white cardboard box in his hand. She saw the boy lift Iz's body by the tail and place him into the box.

Abby didn't wait to see if the boy realized she was gone. She quickly turned and headed down the small gap in the wall, just past the studs. She had no idea where she was or where she was going. The narrow path was dark and dusty, but she had become used to the dark and recalled the advice Iz gave her when she was learning to move about the cage at night. She found a hole that led down to the floor below, and then another to the floor below that.

She quickly ran through the labyrinth of small holes and gaps in the walls, attempting to find the ground and a way out. Her fur was covered in dust and cobwebs. She was tired from constantly moving when she stopped to catch her breath as she entered what seemed like a terminal. A wide open space with numerous clear paths that she could take. As she examined each route, she moved in close to the mouth of the path to see where it might lead. Down one path, she heard numerous human voices. She wanted to avoid humans for sure. One was riddled with debris and seemed more difficult to pass through. As she approached a third route, she noticed something encouraging. A small ray of sunlight. It was not like the dingy room lights; this was bright, beautiful sunlight. Without any further consideration, she set off in that direction.

She made her way through this path, fixated on the sunlight, when she came to a small crack in the wall, beaming with light. She got close and put her nose to it. It smelled amazing. It smelled like freedom. The crack was much too small for her to escape from, however, but as she looked around, she saw where the wooden wall turned to bricks, and between two large bricks was a gap. She headed towards the gap. It would be a tight fit, but tired of looking for new ways out, she decided to try to squeeze through. She pushed her head in and encountered resistance from her midsection. She sucked her stomach in as much as she could and started to make her way through the narrow pass.

As her head cleared the pass and the sunlight hit her face for the first time without the filter of the window, she paused. As she paused, she took as deep a breath of fresh air as she could. It was limited by the rest of her body still being crammed in the passage. At that moment, she felt something strange. She felt something moving inside her. Just a slight movement that wasn't her. It felt funny, and as she noticed it, she immediately knew exactly what it was. "Iz, you fool," she said out loud. Shaking out of the shock of the realization, she pressed forward. She sucked in her stomach one more time and managed to wiggle her way through. She quickly spotted a shaded corner of the building only a few feet away. She quickly scurried to it to catch her breath and decide what to do next.

As she collected her thoughts, she tried to process what she had just realized. As far as timing, this couldn't have been less convenient. Should she turn back? After all, cage or not, there was plenty of food, soft beds, and safety. She wouldn't be lonely;

things there weren't so bad. However, she quickly decided against it. It was a cage. Given how long it took her to get pregnant, what if something happened, then she would be alone in that cage forever. Fate had given her a chance to escape, so she would. Not even for her potential children, but for her.

The shaded corner was the edge of a grassy patch of land. On the other side, she noticed a small wooded area. There was a piece of litter that looked as if it contained some delicious food. That would be her next move. There should be shelter for her, and maybe she could stay in the cover of the woods indefinitely. Especially if there was a frequency of food that happened there.

She started off, hopping through the tufts of grass, taller than her. As she hopped, she could see her destination, but when she hit the ground, all she could see was grass. As she moved, she looked up. She saw the sun. Even though it was going down, its warmth felt so good. It was set against the orange and pink sky, with dark purple clouds scattered about. She pressed forward.

She heard a somewhat familiar sound. Birds were chirping overhead. Without being impeded by the glass and walls, their songs were so clear and lovely. She stopped and looked up, seeing them fly overhead. They seemed so much higher up than they felt from the third-story window. She took one more step and looked up again. She smiled; she was free. Free from the cage, free from the human. She was free from Iz, she felt a little guilty for thinking it, but she was. No more would she have to hold back her thoughts and opinions for fear of upsetting the peace. No more would she have to feel lonely with someone who should be paying her more attention, but most of all, she would no longer have to compete with the wheel. While much of her wished he were still here, she still felt liberated.

As she looked up, she smiled, and she felt light, free. She closed her eyes and took a deep breath. "Goodbye, Iz," she said. Just as she exhaled, a large owl quickly descended on her, whisking her away into the evening sky.

NOTES

_____

_____

_____

_____

_____

_____

_____

_____

_____

_____

NOTES

_____

_____

_____

_____

_____

_____

_____

_____

_____

_____

The Wheel Iz

ABOUT THE AUTHOR

By the numbers alone, Reid was below average in most aspects growing up and would seem to have low potential for any kind of success. With little formal education from a young age and growing up in a low-income home, he had very few examples to reference when it came to the building blocks of success and material security. Regardless, he pressed forward and managed to obtain an education, a respectable career, and build a stable and thriving family, figuring each step out along the way.

In his career, he has focused on one thing: helping normal people achieve more. Whether transitioning family businesses from paper records to software, translating complicated requirements into easy-to-adopt systems, or helping tech companies maximize engagement with the widest possible set of users, he knows that there are human elements that cannot be ignored if you hope to thrive with the average population.

Now, he hopes to share his experiences with those like him, the average young person just trying to figure things out. Career, finance, faith, and relationships are the building blocks for true success, and each is getting more complicated by the day. He is constantly breaking down the basics, hoping to help others implement good frameworks into their lives, with the result being able to define and achieve success on their own terms.

As a father and a big brother, he brings empathetic, but harshly realistic topics to his audience with the sole intention of helping others make their corner of the world just a little bit better.

The Wheel Iz